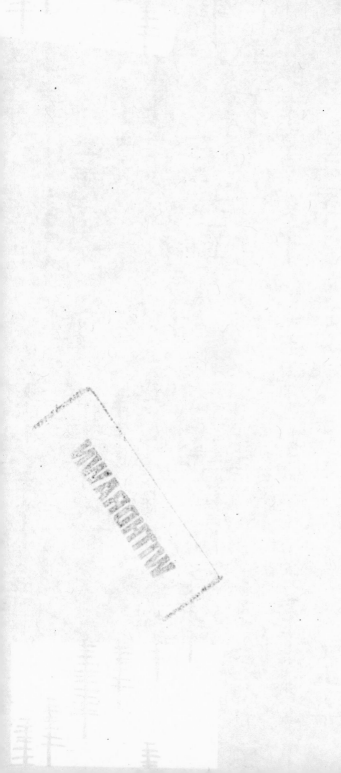

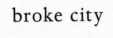

broke city

Wendy McGrath   *a novel*

BROKE

CITY

NeWest Press

Library and Archives Canada Cataloguing in Publication
Title: Broke City / Wendy McGrath.
Names: McGrath, Wendy, author.
Identifiers: Canadiana (print) 20190075090 Canadiana (ebook) 20190075104
ISBN 9781988732732 (softcover) ISBN 9781988732749 (EPUB)
ISBN 9781988732756 (Kindle)
Classification: LCC PS8575.G74 B76 2019 | DDC C813/.6 — dc23

Editor: Douglas Barbour
Book design: Natalie Olsen
Cover photo: Sonja Lekovic
Author photo: Travis Sargent

NeWest Press acknowledges the Canada Council for the Arts, the Alberta Foundation for the Arts, and the Edmonton Arts Council for support of our publishing program. This project is funded in part by the Government of Canada. ¶ NeWest Press acknowledges that the land on which we operate is Treaty 6 territory and a traditional meeting ground and home for many Indigenous Peoples, including Cree, Saulteaux, Niitsitapi (Blackfoot), Métis, and Nakota Sioux.

#201, 8540–109 Street
Edmonton, AB T6G 1E6
780.432.9427
www.newestpress.com

NEWEST PRESS

No bison were harmed in the making of this book.
Printed and bound in Canada   1 2 3 4 5   21 20 19

For John

prologue

Jan grasps the shovel in his right hand. Raises it like a scepter and points its head toward the sky. Then he walks quietly and solemnly across his yard to the pine in the back corner. Its boughs reach over the fence into the alley and as he stands at the foot of the tree he is shrouded in cool darkness. The ground beneath him is a layer of needles and fallen cones that yields as he makes his way closer to the trunk. He looks up. The trunk is a tangled chaos of thin dry little sticks hanging from boughs stiff and brittle and grey. This pine is dying from the inside out. But the scent of pine is still strong and he breathes to reassure himself, not only of this tree's presence but of his own presence. Reassuring himself and the old tree that shelters him and the box. See? We are still here.

Jan buried the box at the foot of this tree. In this box is all of time, all of life, all of his life in his neighbourhood, Santa Rosa. The box is buried at the foot of this old pine tree that is dying from the inside in his backyard. The contents of the box will be his offering to Christine and Fergal, this grieving young couple. His sad promise. But, there is always hope.

He steps on the shovel's head pushing through the pine needles and then the soil underneath gives. Have I done this before? Was it real or was it a dream? Both, he tells himself. He pulls the shovel out of the ground again and pushes down shifting the head of the shovel to lift the cedar box from the ground. But the box resists in the way a sleeping creature might resist waking into sunlight and noise and the sadness of this world, resists leaving behind a cool and deep sleep in the earth under this tree.

Jan smiles at the scent of the cedar box as he lifts it out of the ground. There is the smell of pine and peat and he sees the space left under the tree which he has disturbed and now the tree's roots look like fingers reaching out and away from the fence and toward him.

Still sheltered by the boughs of the pine, Jan sets the cedar box on the ground, brushes the dirt from the top and raises the lid. When he was little, the story of Pandora's Box haunted him. He wants to rewrite the story. Pandora would release happiness into the world instead of sorrow and horror. He would give Pandora only happiness if he could. He would change the story. Instead of sadness, she would have the chance to get back what she had wanted most. Of course, that was impossible. Just as it was impossible for him to get back what he had lost, impossible for Christine to get back the baby.

He lifts the lid of the box. He smells cedar and brandy. He had soaked clean white linen in brandy and wrapped the cake in a shroud before he put it in the box. The cake he made to divide and share with his children, sending it to them with his memories and theirs, is gone. What he had made and sealed inside has become something else. What was inside the box has changed. Jan realizes with a quick intake of breath that what is now in the box is not for him — it is for Christine. He straightens, still holding the shovel, and steps away from the box. There is nothing and everything in the box. He has released objects inside the box, but they are the objects of Christine's memories not of his. Time has transmogrified and a simple cake has turned into something bigger than either him or Christine, but at the same time something that will always be a part of her, a part of Santa Rosa. He does not immediately recognize this collection of objects and yet some part of himself feels he knows these things or has a connection to these things. He knows they are connected to Christine. They disperse into the air, moving in cadence, a murmuration, separate yet part of a grand whole. They hover shining like stars so bright Jan can see them even in daylight.

I

PINE TREE

The house smelled the way it did when the Christmas tree was in the living room. When it was in the corner and still. Frozen with no decorations or lights. It was as if Christmastime had made a mistake and come to the house in the afternoon, in summer when it was hotter inside the house than it was outside. That summer morning, when the house was still cool, Christine's mother had poured the pine-tree-smelling liquid into a silver bucket half-full of hot water. Christine had seen the bottle under the sink and now she could read the label: Pine-Sol.

Pine-Sol was gold and beautiful and when her mother had raised the bottle to screw the cap back on the sun shone through the glass and cast a golden beam of light from the window to the kitchen floor she was about to wash. This must be what heaven looks like,

Christine thought. The smell of pine trees, gold shining on the green and grey tiles in the kitchen and the music playing. That song about golden silence was playing on the radio and Christine thought she might already be in heaven, but maybe no one had told her yet. It was as if pine trees were all around her: the smell of the trees at Elk Island Park on that day she had learned to swim and even her father had come along, and the pine tree in the backyard where she ran to bury the putty discs she had made. She had knelt under its branches then, and the ground was so cool. Christine remembered how it felt, how the needles poked through the thin cotton of her nightdress and stuck to the smooth skin on the tops of her feet and pricked her fingers as she dug in the earth. There was a pine tree in the neighbour's yard too, only the fence separated the two trees. Remembering that moment, it was as if her whole life of seven years had become a life of a hundred years and she felt old and young, and alone and part of her family, as if she were looking at her mother washing the floors through a window. Of course, she thought, this must be what heaven is like. She saw that between the two big yellow words Pine-Sol was a tiny pine tree. Pine-Sol. Pine trees were all around her it seemed, but she wasn't afraid and didn't want to get away. The bottle of Pine-Sol. Heaven could be this simple thing, Christine thought, the scent of the water her mother used to wash floors.

Then the news came on the radio.

*The small community of Shell Lake, Saskatchewan is in
shock this morning...*

Christine's mother rushed to the radio and turned
up the volume.

– What's wrong Mom?

– SHHH!

...as RCMP *investigate the deaths of nine people. The victims,
all members of the same family, were discovered at their
home this morning by a neighbour.* RCMP *are treating these
deaths as homicides. Shell Lake is 50 miles west of Prince
Albert. We will bring you more details about this tragedy as
they become available.*

Christine's mother ran to the phone.

– What's wrong, Mom?

– I'm phoning Gramma.

– Long distance? Christine was shocked. Her mother
   didn't call long distance, especially during the day
   when she said it was so expensive. Christine's mother
   dialed quickly, receiver to her ear, cigarette sticking
   up like an antenna. Christine watched their own
   phone number in the circle at the centre of the dial.

Her mother had written the numbers in blue ink
and each one was a character. The fours were like
sails on boats and the twos were like swans on
the water. Her mother's finger would pierce the
small metal circle inside the bigger metal circle,
go half-way round the dial and return. Again.
Again.

— What's wrong, Mom? Do you know those people,
  Mom? Who are those people, Mom? Does Gramma
  know them? Christine thought about what they'd
  said on the news: *"...the victims, all members of the
  same family..."*

— Is it Gramma?

— No. No, I don't know who it is.

— I'm scared, Mom.

— There's nothing to be scared about.

Christine didn't believe her.

⟨ ⟩⟨ ⟩⟨ ⟩

Her mother had washed all the floors in the house.
The green and grey kitchen tiles, the shiny wood
floors in the living room and the bedrooms and tiny
white square tiles in the bathroom. Christine stood
in the middle of the living room floor watching her

mother crawl with her scrub rag from room to room. She had a burning cigarette between her lips. The wood felt sticky and hot on Christine's bare feet. She stepped back and watched as her footprints disappeared on the floor's surface. She could remember something like this from before. When? She remembered small diamond shapes on the side of a man's socks and how his own footprints followed him from the living room to the kitchen. Was it a dream? Where was her mother in this dream? Christine thought she remembered being in the living room in the little pink house. Her mother had told her to stay there and be quiet. She was afraid to move. She couldn't move. She heard her mother and this man in the kitchen talking, whispering. She didn't move and didn't speak until the man left. Don't move. Don't talk.

◇ ◇ ◇

– Mom, if I showed you a picture of a pine tree would you know what I was talking about, what I mean?

Her mother stopped scrubbing the floor, and still on her hands and knees, turned her head toward her daughter. Christine saw a tiny bead of water trickle down the side of her mother's face as her mouth tightened around her cigarette. She took a drag from it, held it between two wet fingers and flicked the ash into the metal ashtray beside her knee.

– Don't talk nonsense.

– No, Mom, if there weren't words, how would we talk to each other? Would we just draw each other pictures or something?

– I s'pose.

Her mother wiped the sweat from the side of her face with the inside of her wrist, bent to keep the burning end of the cigarette away from her hair.

– But, Mom, if there were no words how would we tell each other what the pictures would mean?

Her mother motioned with a flick of her head.

– Go, go find something to do, I want to get the house cleaned up. I hate coming back to a dirty house.

Her mother made her way to the bathroom, taking the bucket and the bottle of Pine-Sol with her. She set the bottle down beside the toilet and emptied the bucket in the bowl. The toilet gurgled and sputtered like it was flushing itself with no help from anyone else. Christine watched quietly and her mother set down the bucket, sprinkled Comet around the toilet bowl and scrubbed it with a rag made from one of Christine's father's old, worn-out work shirts.

The shirt was green and black plaid. Christine remembered thinking that when her Dad had worn that shirt the pattern was like roads going over and under each other. Roads going to Saskatchewan and back to Edmonton were the only long highway roads she knew. Christine and her family had made that trip so many times...they would go again as soon as her father got home from work. He was taking time off and it was summer, his busiest house-building time Christine was told, so this must be a special trip.

<> <> <>

Christine had left her mother be for a time and now quietly watched her from the bathroom door waiting as her mother squeezed out the rag over the toilet bowl. Christine thought it looked as if she was really trying to hurt something. Her mother stopped and looked up. Christine thought her head looked like an egg in an egg cup.

– Mom, see that picture of a pine tree? If I just showed you the picture would you know what I meant? Christine asked.

– No, I don't know what you mean.

– If I didn't say anything, if I just pointed to the pine tree on that bottle, would you know what I was talking about?

- I honestly don't know what you're talking about
  half the time. You think about things too much.
  It's just a bottle of Pine-Sol.

Her mother poured some of the golden liquid into
the bucket and the pinging sound and the smell made
Christine taste metal. Intense pine, the half-filled
bucket, the water. In that moment, she was lifted
up and, with her eyes closed, she hovered over the
pine tree in the backyard. She could see herself and
her mother talking, having a conversation about...
she knew there was something she wanted to share
with her mother, something she had to ask her but
couldn't find the right words. Her mother started
scrubbing again.

But hadn't she already washed this floor?

〈〉〈〉〈〉

The little green pine tree dangled from the rearview
mirror of their light green Galaxie 500. The little green
tree bobbed when the car hit a bump or a pothole and
it would swing back and forth as they drove out of the
city and down the highway.

- Did you bring the beer? Where's the 26? Her father
  asked quietly and he leaned toward Christine's
  mother, a lit cigarette already in his mouth.

- Yep, the answer stopped in her mother's throat as she inhaled her cigarette at the same time. But, maybe...I don't even think...we shouldn't be going with what's happened.

- Christine, keep that blanket over the beer.

- Can I put my feet on top?

- Yes, just don't move the blanket off the beer.

- Are you hiding it?

- No, her father said. Just keeping it cold.

Her parents looked at each other and smiled. Maybe things were okay. Her sister sat on the other side of the backseat with her blanket and stuffed dog. Her nose was running and she sniffled every now and then.

- Did you give her the Gravol? Christine's father turned from her sister to her mother.

- Yep, just before we loaded up the car.

The cardboard pine tree swung back and forth from the rearview mirror. Tick tock. Tick tock. Her father had bought the pine tree when they stopped for gas on the way out of Edmonton. The gas station on 118th avenue had a sign that was easy to read: **B A**. The **B** in a green tear and the **A** in a red tear and they fit together to make a circle. Through the window,

Christine drew around the outside of the tears and around the whole circle with her finger and said words in her mind: balloon bakery banana barrel bank. She had heard her father one morning before he went to work, when her parents thought she was still asleep.

– You've got me over a barrel...laughing all the way to the bank.

But her mother wasn't laughing.

– We don't have anything in the bank...

Christine stayed under the covers. Don't move. Don't make a sound. She thought about this past winter when that man dropped off a box at their front door. He had thumped on the door and it sounded so loud in the house. Her mother invited him in and left the door open, letting the smell of the winter inside the house. He wore a green uniform.

– Are there toys in there, Mom? Christine asked.

– No. Meat.

– What kind of meat comes in a box?

Christine was making a joke. She thought it would make her mother and the man in the uniform laugh. It didn't. Her father was sitting at the kitchen table, smoking, pretending not to see the man in the uniform.

– It's **SPAM**, her mother said looking from the man
in the uniform to her father. The city's giving people
a box of SPAM.

– For Christmas? Everyone's getting a box of SPAM
for Christmas?

The man in the uniform tried not to look at her mother
and then asked her to sign a piece of paper.

– No, people who have no work in the winter, the city's
giving them a box of **SPAM**.

The man in the uniform made sure to ask for the pen
back. He wore a badge that said: **CITY OF EDMONTON**.
Those words were easy for Christine to read now.
The man turned from the door and he seemed to move
through the cold as if it had weight to it, as if it pressed
around him and his green uniform as he shuffled back
to the still-running van. He got in behind the wheel,
wrote on a clipboard on the dashboard and drove away.

The man that was filling their car with gas at the service
station on 118th Avenue was wearing a green uniform
too. How many green uniforms were there in this world?
This man's uniform had **B A** on a badge on front and
small **B A** badge on his hat.

– Clean your windshield sir? He called her father sir. Sir.

Who was the gas station man, really? What was the story of the gas station man's life? She would never know him, but she could imagine his life as a story. Who would she tell it to? How would she tell it?

When her father had ripped the little pine tree's cellophane wrapping open with his teeth it sounded like breaking glass. He tore a corner off its cover with his teeth, "Puh" and spit the bit of plastic from his mouth out the window, crumpled the rest of the small tree's cellophane cover and threw it after it. With his bit-to-the-quick fingernails, thick fingers with dirt in the cracks of his knuckles he wound the pine tree's green string around the car's rear view mirror. He flicked the little tree like a bug and it swung from side to side. Christine smelled pungent green, pine, but not the same as the smell when her mother washed floors. This pine smell mixed with the smell of cigarettes, and dust, and the warm scent of a dying August.

– Why are you hanging that tree there, Dad?

– Hide the smell of cow shit as we get closer to the farm, hey? He laughed and looked across the front seat at Christine's mother.

– I don't think we should go now, not with what's happened, Christine's mother said.

- A guy who kills that many people is not going to stick around some rinky-dink town. Naw, whoever did it will be long gone.

- Did you know the people who were killed? Christine asked her mother.

- Not really. I think the oldest girl went to school with...no, I don't know them.

- Did you know the people, Dad?

- No, I played ball with their neighbour's cousin though. That family lived out our way.

- I wonder who did it? her mother said.

- Probably some stranger. Some guy passing through.

- Passing through what? There's nothing all the way out there. No, it has to be someone from around.

- Could be a hired hand? Some of those guys are kinda funny...

- You just never know I guess. It gives me a funny feeling that's for sure her mother said, looking out the window.

It was a peculiar time of day. The sun with its last breaths of the day was bright, shining orange as it was disappearing behind the car and shining in the rearview mirror. Christine could smell the

little pine tree in the back seat. She could taste the
smell in the back of her throat and then it travelled
up the back of her head and into the top of her skull.
She didn't want to get car sick. She stuck her head
out the window and closed her eyes against the
thundering sound of the wind. The tight, tart smell
of the ditch weeds and rushing air replaced the green
pine taste at the back of her throat. Green to yellow.

– Do you wanna get your head cut off? Get back
   in the car and roll up the window!

What if I had no head? Would I still be able to see?
Would I know I was in a car and where I was going?
Would I even know what a car was? Could they sew
my head back on? Would I live?

Christine's mother turned toward the backseat and
swatted the air randomly trying to land a slap on
her leg. Christine quickly slammed herself down
in the corner of the backseat. Her mother missed.
Her sister was asleep already in her pyjamas.

– You're damn lucky. Don't stick your head out
   the window again.

The front windows were rolled right down and the
radio blared a song telling her to wear flowers in
her hair if she ever went to San Francisco...but they
weren't going to San Francisco they were going to

Saskatchewan. Then the music and the sound of typewriter keys and the announcer with *Nooow... the news. Police continue their manhunt for the person or persons responsible for the gruesome murders of nine family members from...*

The sun was an aching orange, yellow, red and it reflected like a shot off the rearview mirror. Christine's father had his right hand on the wheel, a cigarette and a stubby brown bottle of Bohemian Maid beer in his left hand. Christine compared the location of her father's hands on the driving wheel to the car clock. His hands made 2 o'clock. The little pine tree was green, the inside of the car was green, the clock was green and it still worked. She knew that it was 7 o'clock. They would change the time when they crossed the Saskatchewan border. There always seemed to be some problem with changing time whenever they went from Edmonton to Saskatchewan or from Saskatchewan to Edmonton. Clocks had to change. Watches had to change. Saskatchewan time or Alberta time. Now she could tell the difference between the changing times. Her father took a drink from the bottle in his left hand.

– Goddammit, this sun is bright he said reaching to adjust the mirror and take a sip from the bottle of beer.

– Look Ma', no hands he said and looked at Christine in the back seat. She laughed.

– Do that again, Dad.

The bright green triangle of the little tree swung back and forth and covering and uncovering red flashing lights in the distance.

– Mounties! Sunnuvabitch!

– How fast were you going? Shit! Gimme the bottle. Quick!

In one motion, Christine's mother shot a cigarette butt into the mouth of his beer bottle. It made a sssssttttt sound before she hung her arm down the side of the car and back-handed the bottle into the ditch. Christine's father slowed the car down and her Mother reached into the back seat and smoothed the blanket over the case of beer.

– Keep your feet on that blanket and keep your mouth shut.

– What's wrong Dad? Were you speeding? Was it the 'Look Ma no hands?'

– Never mind. Just keep quiet.

A Mountie walked out to the middle of the road wearing a red coat with golden buttons and black pants with legs that curved out of his shiny brown boots.

He wore a beige hat and when he motioned Christine's father toward the shoulder of the highway the red sleeves of his coat hit the brown leather pouch at his side.

Her father pulled over to the narrow shoulder where there were already three other cars parked behind the two RCMP cars. The lights on top of the cars flashed red. Christine felt scared. The loose gravel on the shoulder of the highway crunched slowly. In all the trips they had taken on this highway from Edmonton to Saskatchewan, they had never been told to stop by the Mounties.

– What's wrong Dad? Are you in trouble?

– No…quiet.

– Keep your feet on the blanket.

Mounties walked from the parked cars ahead of them to the RCMP cars holding something in their hands. Her father pulled in behind the line of vehicles. The silver water tower in the distance said **HAFFORD**. Christine thought it looked like a silver spaceship, a round circle on top of thick metal legs, a criss-cross of narrow metal for landing gear. Christine imagined they were in a movie. This was an alien invasion and the aliens had come to earth in the Hafford water tower. She worried a lot about aliens invading earth.

Especially at night. Flying saucers. Her grandfather had shown her magazines with actual pictures of UFOs. Her father had said that it was just a hoax but, maybe, it was true after all. This was the alien invasion. **HAFFORD** on the water tower could mean something in the alien language. It could mean Hafford was the half way point to aliens taking over the earth and the Mounties were trying to stop them. Lloydminster was the halfway point on the road to her grandmother's but if you took one of the **L**s from Lloydminster and put it in **HAFFORD** it would be **HALFFORD**. **HAFFORD** already sounded like halfway. Maybe not in alien language, though...

The car in front of them signalled and drove off onto the highway. One of the Mounties motioned with a flashlight for them to drive ahead and fill the spot. Her father turned the radio right down. The Mountie walked over to the car.

– Good evening, sir...ma'am.

The Mountie called her father "sir" too, like the man at the gas station. He called her mother "ma'am." Only men who came to the door to sell things called her mother ma'am.

– Good evening officer her father said. Her father never talked like that.

– Can I see your licence and registration please?

Christine's father fished his wallet from his back pocket while her mother opened the glove compartment and handed a bundle of papers to her father. She craned her neck to look at the Mountie through the driver's side window. Christine's father handed everything over to the Mountie.

– Thank-you sir.

The Mountie touched the brim of his hat and walked to his car, the red light still silently flashing. The Mountie sat in the front seat and Christine could see him leaning over to the centre. Her heart was beating faster. Is the Mountie checking up on her Dad? Maybe the flashlight was also an x-ray gadget that could see through the blanket and he would know there was beer in the car.

– Bet they're looking for the guy who did it.

– Christ, I hope he doesn't smell the beer.

The Mountie brought the papers and driver's licence back to her father.

– Thank-you, sir. He shone his flashlight in the front and back and Christine stayed frozen in the back seat, her feet on top of the blanket, on top of the beer.

- Where'r you heading? the Mountie asked.

- Leask.

- Leask? The Mountie paused. Tipped his hat.

- Well, you folks can be on your way now. Safe
  travelling.

Her father pulled onto the highway and Christine
looked out the back window at the lights, the other
cars pulling over to the shoulder. The HAFFORD
spaceship was getting smaller and smaller. Her mother
pushed in the cigarette lighter, then turned and
reached toward the back seat making a beckoning
motion with her hand.

- Pass me a beer...

Christine pulled back the blanket, took a beer from
the box and leaned forward to hand the bottle to
her mother. She liked the picture on the bottle, the
smiling woman with black hair and a red scarf, and
the drawing of the green leaf beside the woman.
Her mother took the bottle and popped the top off
with the opener on her key chain — which was a
real rabbit's foot. For luck. The little green pine tree
swung from the rearview mirror moving back and
forth to a rhythm that kept softly beating in the back
of Christine's mind.

Don't be scared don't be scared don't be scared.

When she tried to pinpoint one specific thing she feared she couldn't do it. It seemed to be everything and everywhere. Whoever killed those people, UFOs, the Vietnam War. Those three things. Don't. Be. Scared.

⟨⟩⟨⟩⟨⟩

The sky ahead of them was turning black and the sky behind them was orange and red and yellow and bright white. They were driving straight into the mouth of the night and the numbers on the radio and the dials were glowing green and Christine's father was pressing the silver buttons click click click to try to find a station that was in range. In reach. The voices on the Saskatoon station were different the ads for different things and the little bits of noise that came on before the news sounded different than the Edmonton radio station they listened to all the time. Then a blur of sudden white in front of the car and a deadened thud.

— What the hell...?

— Shit, must've been a bird.

— My grandma said if a white bird flies in front of you it means a death in the family.

— Do you think it's dead? Christine asked.

– If it isn't I sure as hell stunned the little bugger, her father said.

– Who will die, Mom?

– No one, it's just an old wives' tale.

– That bird's number was sure up...

Her parents laughed low and soft not like the sound
of real laughing but laughing without opening
their mouths. Then they were quiet. Smoking their
cigarettes and drinking from their bottles of beer
looking straight ahead into the white light created
by their car, bright and ominous. White broken lines
double solid lines where cars were not allowed to
pass. Tap tap tap her father's cigarette on the lip of
the ashtray. A louder tap tap tap as insects seemed
to propel themselves straight toward their car.
The radio playing Bobbie Gentry. Her father cut
the silence.

– What did the bug say when it hit the wind shield?
If I had the guts, I'd do it again.

They all laughed, except her sister who seemed to
be sleeping through everything on this trip.

⟨⟩⟨⟩⟨⟩

Two deep ruts formed the path to the porch of her grandmother's house and the headlights of their car pushed their way through the night-blue darkness around them. The sky was painted with stars, why were there so many more stars here than there were in the city?

Christine wanted to be first out of the car, so excited to see her grandmother. Her father hadn't turned off the car, the headlights would light the way to the back door as he carried the beer to the house. Her mother was carrying her sleeping sister. The radio blared into the night. Dogs barked. Christine stopped. The bird was stuck to the grill of the car. It was a white bird. Its eyes were closed and its beak was wide open as if it might have been trying to call out to the other birds, warning them to stay away from this car, this family.

— Dad.

Christine pointed to the bird. Surprised there was not more blood. The headlights cast the small thing's grotesque shadow, it seemed much larger as its distorted shape seeped on to the hood of the car.

— Goddammit! Probably cracked the grill, her father said and spit.

— What are you going to do with it, Dad?

— It's not going anywhere. Scrape it off tomorrow.

Christine could feel the lights and the shadows on her face at the same time, saw bugs flying in the car lights. The bird's feet dangled from under it.

— If it had the guts, it'd do it again! her father laughed.

The bare light above the back door with moths flapping and bashing themselves against the glass. If they had the guts…

Her mother opened the door, the dogs barked, and her sister didn't wake.

— You made it I guess, Christine's grandmother shouted over the dogs, hugging her mother and smoothing her sister's hair.

— Mom, you're not even locking your door?

— Well, I knew you were coming…

— We could have been anybody. They still haven't caught the guy. We were stopped outside Hafford…

— If somebody wants to come get me, well, it's my time I guess…you can put the little one in the back bedroom. Her grandmother kissed the top of Christine's sister's head.

— That's just nonsense…

Christine's father followed behind Christine, holding the beer box like a suitcase.

– You hit something, Christine's grandmother said, holding the door open and shading her eyes against headlights, as if the beam had the hurt of bright sunlight.

– Yeah, goddam bird...

Christine's grandmother bent to give her a hug and kiss her cheek.

– Hello girlie, she said. Christine took one last look at the crumpled bird and went inside.

Christine's father stepped past her grandmother.

– I hope they catch the guy soon, her grandmother said as her mother closed the bedroom.

Still her sister slept.

– Everyone's looking at each other and wondering "Is it you?" It's a terrible feeling, just terrible. It could be one of us.

– You should be locking your door, Mom.

– Are you hungry? I've got a pot of coffee on the stove.

– I'll have a beer first.

– I don't want you to drink alone, Christine's father
  said, taking a beer from the box by the sink.
  He popped the cap using the metal bottle opener
  attached to the side of the counter. This bottle
  opener was familiar to Christine. She remembered
  the opener always being there. It said "Coca-Cola."
  Her mother opened a bottle too, and her father
  made a clicking sound with the side of his mouth,
  winked at her mother as she drank from the squat
  bottle. Christine thought her grandmother looked
  sad. Only for a second.

– Where's Daddy?

– Downtown.

– He should be here protecting you instead of at
  the beer parlour with his drinking buddies.

– Phht...don't think he'd be much protection,
  her grandmother laughed and lit a cigarette.

– Pass me that?

Her mother touched the lit cigarette to hers and drew
her breath in and out. Her cigarette burned red at the
end. She blew smoke toward the ceiling and Christine
followed its trail to the sepia-tinged shape above the
kitchen table. The smoke from so many cigarettes
had made a map on the ceiling and the capital city

was the bare bulb. Christine stared. Where was this map's legend? What would the light bulb symbol mean? The bulb cast a strange light in the kitchen. Like the way the headlights had shone on the poor dead bird.

— What will you do with the bird, Dad? Christine asked quietly.

— I'll put it in the garbage tomorrow.

— Can we bury it?

— Worry about it tomorrow. C'mon get to bed, her mother said to Christine. Go wash up. Scoot.

— Can't I stay up a little later? It's summer holidays...

— Half an hour. Go watch TV.

Her grandmother hadn't turned off the TV when they got there. No need to "warm up the idiot box" as her father said. Christine sat in her grandmother's worn red velvet chair while the grown-ups were in the kitchen. She could see her grandmother standing at the counter, flicking ashes into a small metal ash tray resting on the lip of the sink. There was a movie on TV. It might have been in colour but her grandmother had a black and white TV, so there was no way to be sure. The title was *The Family Way* and Hayley Mills was in it. Of all the actors with English accents, Hayley Mills was one of her favourites. There was another one who looked like her in *The Three Lives of Thomasina*. The cat died in that movie. Stiff as a board. Christine tried to sit quietly, stiff as a board in the chair, but she could see her grandmother's detective magazines in a pile on the arborite coffee table, along with another metal ash tray with a few cigarette butts in it, her grandmother's liquid embroidery tubes in a plastic bag and the table cloth she was doing, with a wooden hoop circling a cluster of pine cones attached to a sparse branch. Christine could hear the conversation in the kitchen and tried to concentrate on Hayley Mills' accent but the talk in the kitchen kept breaking into her.

– The whole family's gone. The whole family. Bodies in the yard...in the house...shot while they slept in their own beds. Who could even think up such a thing? The baby was found outside with the mother, I guess...the little thing shot as she held it right in her arms. She must have seen the guy coming. She must've tried to run.

– But how far could you run with a baby in your arms?

– Gone just like that.

On the floor beside the chair was a pile of *True Detective Stories* magazines. The top half of the covers

were missing, but Christine saw the name on the page underneath. She picked up the first magazine on the pile and opened it to a random page and read: "...she screamed again and again as the depraved maniac cut into the soft flesh of her thighs..."
In that moment, Christine wished she hadn't learned to read. She pictured the girl, the screams, the blood...

Christine went to bed without being asked. She didn't want to hear any more talking. She'd quickly rinsed her face to get into the safety of the bed and get to sleep so the adults would be awake to protect the house. Some soap had gotten into her eyes and she blinked against the sting, rubbing her eyes with the corner of the warm pillow case. Christine's body and her thoughts remained in the kitchen as she listened to her mother and her grandmother talking. She was waiting for something to make her feel safe. She felt as if she were imagining herself there in bed and waited for something that would make her feel like her body and her thoughts were real again. What if someone broke into the house right now? Killed them all. She pinched herself. The plastic curtains moved against the window with a sigh.

〈〉〈〉〈〉

Christine awakened and heard footsteps. A click.
Light under the door. Silence.

- That's the fifth time she's checked if the door's
  locked, her mother whispered to her father in
  the other bed.

- Whoever it is…we could know him.

- Some nut on the loose…no one from around
  here…

⟨⟩⟨⟩⟨⟩

Christine woke up the next morning, she heard
her mother's and her grandmother's voices in the
kitchen. She lay in bed and thought: I am still alive.
The Vietnam War hadn't come to Canada, UFOS
didn't come to get me, and nobody's killed me.

The morning gently pulled the plastic curtain in
and out from the window screen. It might be okay
in the end. She crawled over her sleeping little sister
and stood on the bedroom floor. It was already
warm against the soles of her feet. Spikes of green
and pine cones worn dull and shabby led her to
the kitchen.

II

The heavy air smelled a mix of burnt hair and something rancid. Frying fat. Christine's mother closed the windows.

– What stinks?

– Those damn meat plants. The wind is blowing in our direction.

But when Christine's mother struck a match to light a cigarette, the flame was still and as she drew breath from the cigarette the thin snake of smoke slithered straight up to the ceiling. Disappeared.

– I hope the wind blows the other way soon, Christine said.

The dad of the family who lived in the house across the alley worked at one of the meat-packing plants. Christine didn't know which one exactly. Sometimes Christine would see him carrying a cardboard box into the house across the alley after he worked a day shift at the plant. Christine's friend told her most of the time he brought home hamburger, but sometimes he brought home steaks. Christine asked what her friend's father did at the plant and she said he worked in the *abattoir*. Christine thought it must be like a fancy ballroom where there were shining chandeliers that cast a yellow light on everything. There was probably music playing. Her friend's father came home from work wearing a clean white shirt and black pants. Christine remembered once, when she waited in the porch at her friend's house, she had seen a small red smear on her friend's father's shoe. She remembered a bright red cut on her mother's foot once a long time ago and how a sad, dangling piece of ripped white lace seemed to reach toward it to blot the blood and make it disappear. A fear, a sadness came over Christine. She pictured her mother that morning: tired-looking and, now she remembered, scared.

The meat-packing plants were near her neighbourhood, Santa Rosa. Christine's mother said they lived in Packingtown. Santa Rosa sounded better. Rosa meant rose. It was the name of a saint and roses smelled better than the air from the packing plants. Sundays, they drove to church along 66th street, toward Fort Road and the Transit Hotel. Christine loved to look at the tall tower in the Canada Packers stockyard. Beautiful red brick with a grey ring at the top. Did her friend's father go up there? She couldn't see any stairs or steps or even a ladder. Someone could get trapped in there.

Maybe her friend's father. More likely a beautiful princess, right here in Packingtown. "Rapunzel, Rapunzel…let down your hair." If the wind from the packing plants was blowing in the direction of the tower, Christine was pretty sure Rapunzel would hate the smell too. In her book of fairy tales, Rapunzel dangled her hair out of a window in a tower and let a prince climb up it to free her. That would hurt. Even when her mother brushed the knots out of her hair and pulled strands to braid it, it hurt. She did like having braids in her hair though. Christine liked to run her hands over the braids, rippling smooth and thick and then tapering to a point like a paintbrush. Christine knew there was a world far beyond Santa Rosa, beyond their green city but sometimes she felt like Rapunzel. She was alone and looking down on everything that went on around her: her father and mother, her sister. Sometimes she felt as if her parents were far away even when they were in the same house, talking in a language she didn't understand. That didn't make sense when she thought about it. She knew the words they were saying and, if anyone asked, she would be able to tell them what each one meant on its own. One. By. One. Why was it, then, that when her parents talked they seemed to mean something else, something she couldn't quite catch. A word, or a maybe it was a picture, the blueprints her father looked at sometimes, that everyone else seemed to understand but her. One day, Christine would paint

herself out of Santa Rosa and into that bigger world
she knew must be out there. Beautiful colours
that she would use to create a story of her own.
She would write it and she would colour it whatever
way she wanted and she would know exactly what
everything meant because she would say it first.
What to say and when to say it.

– Will you braid my hair, Mom?

– Okay, run and get an elastic and the tail comb.

Christine pulled open the drawer in the bathroom.
A tube of Brylcreem, tube of toothpaste, jar of
Noxzema, and two twisted red elastics with pieces
of her dark brown hair snarled around them from
the last time she pulled them out of her hair.
The black tail comb. There was her father's can of
shaving cream, but not his silver razor. It was on the
shelf in the medicine cabinet. It must be dangerous.
KEEP OUT OF REACH OF CHILDREN.
Why was "THE" missing? That was wrong and it
was written on so many things. Drano and pink baby
aspirins and Comet powder and Pine-Sol and bleach.
There were so many things that were out of the reach
of children. But Christine knew where the razor
rested, clean and shiny on the shelf where her father
left it to dry. She knew the blades were right beside it,
in their own little box like some mysterious treasure.
She would watch her father shave but she had never

told him or her mother that once she had climbed
up on the vanity and taken down the small box of
razor blades and the razor. That one time, she had
gripped the razor the way her father did and was
surprised how heavy it felt. She slowly, secretly,
slid a paper-wrapped silver blade from the box.
The paper made a quiet scraping sound. The blade
inside was so light and so thin. How could something
that weighed nothing be so dangerous? Keep out of
reach of children. There was always something to
be afraid of. She slowly returned the blade to its box
and set it back beside the razor, making sure every
item faced the same way as before.

Christine put the elastic knot on the table beside her
mother's ashtray. Her mother looked at the them and
sent a stream of smoke toward the ceiling. She set the
cigarette on the metal ashtray and moved it to the
opposite side of the table. The smoke slithered toward
Christine.

— Turn around her mother said and made a circle
   with her index finger.

— Don't pull too hard okay, Mom?

— Just want to make sure there are no stray hairs.

Christine felt the comb's teeth scrape against her forehead, her temples, over her ears as her mother gathered her hair in one hand at the base of her neck.

– Your hair's so thick.

– Someone could climb up on it.

– What?

– Rapunzel. Rapunzel, must have had thick hair. How long would it take me to grow my hair that long?

– Years. I think hair stops growing at some point anyway. No one can live a fairy tale.

– It's a good story though.

Her mother's cigarette burned away in the ashtray, strands of smoke weaving themselves in the air and disappearing. Christine could feel her mother pulling in sequence — 1 – 2 – 3 — on the lengths of her own hair, moving her hands in invisible circles that conjured a braid half-way down the length of her spine.

– Fairy tales make me think of real life sometimes. Rapunzel's in a tower…there's a tower at Canada Packers…

– A smoke stack, her mother laughed. Christine hardly ever heard her mother laugh, especially at things she said. She didn't know this joke either.

— Well, it looks like a tower. Is that where the stink is coming from?

— Some of it must...

— Is that where Brenda's Dad works?

— At Canada Packers? Yep, Andy works regular shift work and gets a regular paycheque...

Christine could sense her mother's hands moving faster as she got closer to the end of the braid, the narrowest part. She heard the snap of the elastic and out of the corner of her eye saw her mother stretch it wide open with the fingers of her right-hand reach behind her head and

snap snap snap

coil it around the tip of the braid.

— There.

She held Christine by the shoulders and turned her around to face her. Her mother took a drag from her cigarette and blew smoke to the floor like she was playing the flute. Christine had seen a flute player on TV. It was jazz. "Take Five" was the name of the song. She and her mother were taking five.

- Mr. Vanderveen works on the floor with Brenda's Dad.

- The floor?

- The kill floor.

- Brenda calls it an *abattoir*.

- Same thing.

- What is it? Christine thought she knew. Her throat was getting tight and her stomach felt as tight as the elastic on the end of her braid.

- That's where the animals are killed.

- What animals?

- Cows, pigs...

- Who kills them?

- The workers.

- Mr. Vanderveen? Mr. Vanderveen and Brenda's Dad kill the animals?

- I don't know exactly what he does, I've never really asked...her mother's voice trailed off distractedly. She licked her fingers and smoothed the stray hairs at Christine's temples. Christine could smell the faint remnants of cigarette smoke. She felt sick.

- I think Brenda's Dad might kill the animals. I saw blood on his shoe once.

- It's part of his job then.

- Do you think it's animal blood?

- Well what else would it be?

- I saw some blood on your foot once.

Her mother stared straight at her.

- You imagined it.

- No, I didn't. I saw it. That time in the morning.

Christine remembered blue. A piece of lace ripped
and trailing above a cut on her mother's foot. Blood.

- You must be thinking of something else.

What? That drive-in movie with Julius Caesar and
Brutus? The knives and blood she couldn't forget.

- No. It wasn't that Mom. I remember.

- Okay, that's enough of that. You have such an
  imagination. You've got to stop thinking about
  those kinds of things. Do you want to read a book?
  C'mon we'll go read a book.

Smiling, her mother trapped her cigarette between
her fingers, took a drag and cradled the ashtray
in her palm as she walked to the living room.
Christine's sister played with plastic farm animals
on the hardwood floor. There were cows and pigs
and sheep…Christine thought of Brenda's Dad
and Mr. Vanderveen on the kill floor standing
in blood wearing nice clean white shirts. No,
it couldn't be true. Any of it. Her sister clutched
a little brown plastic cow. *Chez Hélène* was on TV.
"…*écoutez bien mes petits amis*…"

Her mother patted the chesterfield and opened
the book of fairy tales and nursery rhymes.
It was a big heavy book that was frayed along the
edges and the corners of the fading green cover.
Christine sat beside her mother and her sister
sat on her mother's lap.

– Now what should we read…

– Rapunzel.

Christine's sister said Rapunzel too and leaned
her small head into her mother.

III

"Your-dad's-side-of-the-family" lived in a basement suite not far away from Christine's small house in Santa Rosa. They were going there for Christmas Eve and the leaving couldn't come fast enough. She tried looking out the living room window, but it was covered with frost. She knew by heart what was outside: the big trees lining their street, leafless, cold and solemn and the church down the street with its stained-glass windows. They were like the church's very own Christmas lights. Christine still had hopes for this day, Christmas Eve. Wasn't that what Christmas was all about? Hope? That's what everyone was saying on TV anyway.

Christine thought their TV was beautiful. It rested on a wire frame like something in a museum. When she put her hands on the warm screen and spread her fingers she was part of this beautiful object. "Warm up the idiot box," her father would say. But when Christine turned on the TV she knew it was not an idiot box. Its name was Sylvania. It was Sylvania's box. The TV was turquoise and beige and it was like a spaceship control made from the velvet gown of a regal princess in a knights-in-shining-armour movie.

Sylvania also made her think of sylvan, where the trees were thick with green leaves in the summer. Summer had the longest day and December had the longest night. But it seemed like today was the longest day after all. She was waiting for something good to happen on Christmas Eve. Sure, Santa was coming tonight after she went to sleep, but something good to happen besides that. If anything good would happen before that, it would have to be at her father's-side-of-the-family.

Her parents did not seem to have the same hope as Christine.

That morning, Christine got up in the quiet dark and plugged in the Christmas tree. She knelt in front of it. The colours from the lights shone on the walls and turned the living room walls into stained glass. The scent of pine defined that one small moment and that one place in the house. The tree had turned into something else, something that she didn't even have a name for anymore. She would give it a new name. Not pine tree. Not Christmas tree. This new name might not even be an actual word, but something beyond a word. A shape or the taste of scribbled green needles and painted branches growing from an invisible place and sap escaping from the rough bark —

all of those things became part of her. She could taste the green and she gathered it in as if the rest of the day depended on the taste of this moment right now. There was a yellow plastic star at the top of the tree and Christine closed her eyes and imagined she could fly above that moment, above that star, and above the snow and the cold and the puffs of white coming out of the chimneys of the houses in Santa Rosa and find a green city with grass you could see and feel in every season, even winter, and that was full of trees like their Christmas tree and smelled this beautiful all the time and everywhere. She closed her eyes and tried to hold on but the moment and the feeling and the word-not-a-word was gone. She felt the tops of her feet cold against the floor. She stood and shook her legs walking silently back to her room. Christine's sister woke while she searched in a drawer for her green socks and pulled them on. Better. "Come on, it's Christmas Eve!" Christine said to her sister. "Let's go have our breakfast." "Happy Christmas Eve," her sister said. "Happy Christmas Eve!" and they both cheered.

Her mother made Christine and her sister cream of wheat. It was Christmas Eve and her mother told them it was a happy tradition, but Christine couldn't remember ever having it on Christmas Eve and when her mother closed the cupboard door to put back the box of cereal, Christine noticed it was the only cereal on the shelf. Christine slowly stirred the brown sugar and white cream of wheat in the bowl. The white snow of winter mixed with the sand on the streets with the spoon making tracks to her grandmother's place for Christmas Eve.

Christine's mother filled the glass coffee percolator with water and measured coffee into the metal hat on the glass tube inside. The coffee smelled good and the dark liquid began travelling up and through the glass tube. Christine heard her father in the bathroom shaving. The quick back and forth splash of the razor in the sink as he rinsed the shaving foam off the blade.

When her father came to the breakfast table he was dressed in his good shirt and trousers. His face was smooth and shiny and his hair was combed. "How are my girls?" he said to Christine and her sister. "Happy Christmas Eve, Dad!" Christine said. "When are we going to the dinner?"

"Later this afternoon. Not too early...not too late," and he laughed.

Christine's mother unhooked a green Melmac cup from inside the cupboard and put it on the table in front of her father. She filled it with coffee and the steam rose like a ghost.

— Thank you kindly, he said in a loud, cheerful voice. He put three teaspoons of sugar in the cup and poured in evaporated milk from a tin that had two open triangles on opposite sides of the lid. He slurped as he drank from the cup.

— Bah. You didn't rinse the soap out of the cup! Are you trying to poison me?

— What are you talking about? I rinse the dishes 'til they squeak!

— I taste soap.

— You're imagining it. She took a sip of black coffee in her cup. Tastes fine to me. Christine's father got up and poured the coffee down the sink.

— I'll get my own coffee. At least I know what's in it.

— What are you putting on such a show for in front of the kids?

— You guys know Daddy's just joking around, don't you?

— Are you trying to poison Dad? Christine asked her mother.

– Don't be so silly. 'Course not. Your Dad's imagining things again.

– Again? Hm. Her mother lit a cigarette.

– Boy, you sure look dressed up today. How come you don't hide at the beer parlour and come home pissed when we go to your-side-of-the-family for Christmas?

Her father laughed in a low, mean way and smirked as he brought his cigarette to his mouth. He screwed up his face at her mother as he inhaled.

– I don't drink any more...but I don't drink any less. He laughed. Christine's mother wasn't laughing.

– If you think you're putting on a good show for your mother, don't bother. She knows exactly what you do. She just pretends everything's fine.

– And just exactly what do I do? Huh? What do I do?

– I'm not arguing with you.

– You think you're so smart. You tell me, what do I do?

– Nothing. Absolutely nothing. Let's just go and pretend everything's okay, at least for your mother.

Christine decided she would pretend too. She would pretend she couldn't hear her parents. It made her feel better, like everything was going to be okay in the end. She looked at her sister who had stopped eating her cream of wheat to stare at her parents and made a silly face. Her sister smiled and Christine mouthed a "Happy Christmas Eve…"

〈 〉〈 〉〈 〉

They didn't have far to drive to her grandparents' place. They lived too far to walk, especially in winter, at night, but her father's-side-of-the-family lived in the same part of the city: North East.

〈 〉〈 〉〈 〉

They parked in front of the house and Christine could see the windows of her grandparents' basement suite were covered in a layer of frost too. Why did the windows in her house and her grandparents' house seem always to be the only windows covered with ice in the winter? Nobody could see in and nobody could see out. The Christmas lights framing the shape of the window were only watery colours, blurred and diffuse as if they actually were under water. Green and red and blue.

Bright little fish trapped under ice. No one looking in would be able to tell there was a family in the basement suite of the house. They were invisible and having an invisible Christmas Eve. Invisible happiness. Something was behind the ice and Christine didn't know what could be hibernating in that hidden basement suite.

The sidewalk was scattered with gravel and her heavy boots made a scraping sound in the quiet night. Christine looked up and wondered why the windows on the main floor of the house her grandparents rented were clear and bright. Another family rented the main floor. She could see their Christmas tree in the window high above her as she and her family walked toward the stairway leading down to the basement of the house where her grandparents lived. The main floor family's Christmas tree had lights that blinked on and off and made the silver tinsel hanging perfectly from every pine branch shine.

<> <> <>

When the family that lived upstairs walked the floor squeaked. Christine could hear the rhythm of their steps heels-toes-one-two-three-one-two-three. Pause.

Maybe they were dancing up there. But she never heard any music and, really, Christine didn't think they were the dancing types. She had watched out the window from below ground level and seen the various family members coming or going up or down the front concrete stairs holding on to the black wrought iron railings then along the front walk: the mother and father and their two daughters were unsmiling trudgers. The oldest daughter looked nice though. She kept her head up when she walked and had pretty clothes. She wore high heels. Where did the main floor family all go when they left the place above her grandparents? Once, Christine and her grandmother had seen the oldest daughter at Northgate Mall when it was new and her grandmother had said "Hello." The daughter was all dressed up. She was wearing a matching pink skirt and jacket and her hair was all backcombed. She smiled when she said "Hello" back to Christine's grandmother. It was a strange kind of surprise to see this daughter out in the green city. This daughter now seemed part of the world of taking the bus to go shopping and spend money on things you don't really need — just for the odd treat every now and then. That day Christine's grand-mother had bought her pink elephant popcorn with a prize in the box. That whole day was pink. So, when they ran into the oldest daughter that day her outfit seemed to match the very air Christine was breathing.

Here was a person who was part of another life living alongside hers. She was not just hearing the daughter as part of the anonymous soft thumping overhead when she visited her grandmother she was right here with her in this world. When the people living upstairs ran the Mixmaster, the TV set danced in time to the electric current being used. But there wouldn't be TV on tonight anyway. The TV wasn't turned on for Christmas Eve.

〈〉〈〉〈〉

Christine stood in the doorway and imagined they had jumped into an aquarium. She had watched the fish swim around in the big tank in her school library. A box of water. Warm bubbling water. The fish were so colourful and their fins billowed in the water. They were like the fish: swimming in cigarette smoke thickening in the basement suite, mouths opening and closing to talk, to eat, to exhale cigarette smoke, to yawn. The Christmas tree in the corner was like the little green pine tree in the corner of the aquarium. It was as if Christine and her family were all swimming around the tree as her father closed the door to the basement. Her grandmother popped her head around the corner from the tiny kitchen.

– You're here then.

Christine's mother took their coats and piled them on her arms before hanging them over the coats already hanging on mismatched metal hooks by the door.

Everyone would be allowed to open one present after supper was finished and all the dishes were done. No presents before the dishes were done. Don't start. Don't even ask. The roaster could be abandoned to soak, but only the roaster because the turkey skin always stuck to the bottom. After supper, Christine's grandmother would open her present wearing the red-trimmed apron that had pictures of kitchen utensils on it. When her dad and uncles sat back in the chairs with tooth picks in their mouths and all the tattered paper was balled up and thrown on the floor it was like the little rainbow-coloured stones on the bottom of the aquarium.

— How long will supper be? her father shouted toward the kitchen.

Her aunt made herself a drink of rum and coke. Two ice cubes in a beautiful glass that changed from white to gold. Lines of cold bubbles racing to the top of the glass. She smoked Rothman's cigarettes with the blue and silver package. The smell of rum and coke meant movie star to Christine and when her aunt put the cigarette in the locomotive ashtray Christine had bought her grandmother (she didn't smoke but it made a nice decoration when everyone else's cigarette smoke came out of the top) there was a ring of red lipstick on the filter.

– Thanks for the invitation, don't mind if I do, her father said as he made a rum and coke for himself in a glass much bigger than her aunt's.

– You could at least wait until you've eaten, Christine's mother said to him under her breath.

– Just getting into the Christmas spirit. Her father was smiling anyway.

Then her aunt and uncle stood in the kitchen doorway and sang "O Tanenbaum" as a surprise for her grandparents on her father's side. To Christine, is sounded like "snick snack Bisto." She guessed it had something to do with Christmas Eve gravy. She didn't ask what it really meant. It was like everyone was under some... kind...of...spell. Everyone was quiet. Everyone was being happy.

– Come to the table, her grandmother said, looking as if Christmas was a serious concern.

They shuffled around in the tiny kitchen, a mish-mash of tables covered by two table cloths with Christmas trees on them and then sat and shuffled some more on chrome and folding chairs. Christine's sister sat on an empty wooden mandarin orange box. Everything was boxes and squares. Green and brown tiles on the floor. Dark brown cupboards with little square handles.

A square wooden table and two card tables set up and added to the ends left and right. Boxes on the shelf above the white gas stove: spice tins, a box of cream of tartar, baking soda, Bisto. The story of the food they were eating could be read from left to right on that kitchen shelf. On the table, there was barely any room for the plates and knives and forks because her grandmother had set down so much food. Steam rose from heaping mismatched bowls and plates: mashed potatoes, cabbage rolls, perogies, peas, sausage, turkey, stuffing, homemade sauerkraut and pork hocks, pickles, and a duck Christine's grandfather had shot himself. Her grandmother had gutted and plucked it and cooked it. Christine didn't like the look of the meat on the plate.

— Will I like it? she asked her grandfather.

— It'll put hair on your chest.

She definitely wasn't eating any duck. Her grandmother
was hovering over the table and waving her arms.

– Pass the bowls this direction, clockwise, clockwise,
   or someone's going to miss something!

– Sit down and eat, Mom! Christine's father said.

In that moment, Christine imagined her father as
a once-upon-a-time little boy, always calling her
grandmother "Mom" and, maybe, even crying. But
everyone was laughing and dishing up their plates,
so, maybe it was only her who was feeling sad, sad,
that a lot of time had passed and people would all get
old one day. People wouldn't matter as much. The
bowls went around the table. Christine sat beside her
aunt watching her red painted fingernails as she cut
her food and then brought the fork to her lipstick-red
mouth. She tried to mimic her actions, her manners.
The way she held her fork with a straight finger
anchoring the top, the way she only moved her knife
in short, back-and-forth motions, not like a hacksaw
cutting a 2×4. Christine's aunt handed her the small
platter of duck.

– Got it? she said as Christine slid her hand under
   the platter and used the serving fork to put two
   small pieces of meat on her own plate. Christine
   let go and her aunt passed the platter to her uncle.

Christine had never tasted duck before. She cut a tiny piece and put it in her mouth, making sure she didn't bite the tines of the fork, just the meat. She didn't like the duck at all. It tasted the way she imagined the water it swam in might taste, maybe it was supposed to taste like that.

Christine kept on chewing and looking around the table: her grandmother was sitting beside her grandfather now, her sister was perched on a telephone book on the wooden box on the chair beside her mother, her aunt and uncle concentrated on their plates. Now all of them were swimming on top of the aquarium, like that duck must have done before her grandfather shot it, feeling the wind and the sunshine and knowing that there was a world that existed under the surface of the water, where things moved and lived and died.

— Jesus Christ! her father yelled and pulled a piece of food out of his mouth, wiping his finger on the side of his plate.

— There's still some shot in this goddamn duck! He made spitting motions with his mouth and pushed his chair from the table with a scraping sound.

— Jesus Christ! Is everyone trying to poison me? He wiped his mouth and stomped out of the kitchen.

– Her mother and grandmother: What's wrong? What's the matter?

Christine pushed her chair from the table.

– Sit down, her mother said.

– I'm going with Dad.

She ran to the front door.

– Dad, can I come with you?

– No, stay inside. I'm just going for a walk.

– But, I want to come with you. I can keep you company? What's wrong?

Christine's coat had fallen off the hook and onto the floor. She picked it up and grabbed the mittens that had been packed inside one of the sleeves. She slammed her feet into her boots and ran after her father.

– Can I come with you? Please, Dad?

– I don't care then, come if you want.

– Christine, get back in here! her mother shouted.

– I'm going for a walk with Dad… and she slammed the frozen, frosted door and all of them inside became invisible.

The air was a knife. The zipper on her coat wasn't closed. The night reached for her neck, for her ears…

Christine ran to keep up with her father. Her coat flapped in the wind and her mittens weren't tucked completely into the cuffs of her jacket. The wind cut like tight strings around her wrists. Her skirt bunched underneath the jacket and her favourite white tights with the tiny circles that made tiny diamonds were wrapping the winter around her legs.

Her father had the collar of his long tweed coat turned up and he puffed on the cigarette in his mouth. His hair was still its shiny black, with a Brylcreem swirl on his forehead. He had shaved. Today was special, Christine still thought that. He had his hands shoved into the pockets of his coat. Christine had wished he would hold her hand so she could keep up with him better, but he looked straight ahead. She wondered if she had failed in some way at something. She didn't know what to say to him.

– Do you believe in Santa, Dad? I do.

She was running to keep up and her breath was puffing out into the dark cold.

– I think it's important to believe in something. Can I walk with you Dad?

- I just want to get some fresh air. Go back to
  the house.

But he had set out with no hat and his tweed dress
coat was unbuttoned against the cold. He had his
collar up. He stopped, cupped his hands and lit a
cigarette. The red flame of the match lit his face and
Christine thought it was like a halo. He held the
cigarette between his lips puffing in and out without
having to touch the cigarette. His hands were in
his pockets and his shoulders hunched. Christine
struggled to keep up with him. Her mother called
her. Brittle sound into the still winter night. She
kept running beside her father and every time she
pulled her hood up over her head, it fell back off,
bouncing as she ran. The white vapour of her words
were ghosts.

- Do you believe in Jesus, Dad? That's what
  Christmas is about, right Dad?

But he said nothing. It was as if she weren't even
there. She was invisible now. Her father wasn't seeing
her at all. Where was he? She thought, he does not
belong here in this time, in this place. Her father
seemed another person entirely. Someone she didn't
know. For a moment, she didn't recognize him, had
never really seen him before. Who was this man?

She ran to keep up with her father, this ghost, as they travelled down the street with the wire-fenced barbed-wire railway yards in sight. The wind sock was straight out like someone was tipping their hat. A clown. She hated clowns. They weren't funny. The night was inky black, and the stars were everywhere. You could see every star in the galaxy, the universe, and Christine knew it would take until she died to count them all.

Christine dreams:

*A heart-shaped potato. Two broken eggs on the floor
each with a double-yolk. A teabag without tea.
A five-leaf clover. A red rose. Small plates go on top of
larger plates not on top of bowls. Here are some stories:
a pile of letters, a rolled-up newspaper, strangers singing
Christmas carols, snow. Sounds like you made that
up. Inside a church with rich, dark, wood, and green-
patterned carpet. Upstairs to watch a singer rehearse.
Downstairs to sit in an empty pew that changes to a
chair. Then an old house all alone in a field at the end
of a long driveway. At the beginning of the driveway
are tall pine trees. Looking from a low angle they seem
huge. The house is not a good feeling. Someone who is
her but not her is crying.*

The green cotton uniform her aunt used to wear
for Phys Ed class was folded in Christine's drawer.
Her aunt had hated Phys Ed as much as she'd hated
the uniform, so she'd given it to her. The uniform
had buttons down the front, a belt that buttoned
in the front and a pocket. It had short sleeves and
gathered short legs that her aunt said were like
bloomers. Christine thought the uniform was the
closest she could get to high school fashion.

She envisioned high school as a place where teenagers
stood around lockers, had lunch in the cafeteria and
went on dates. They also would drive around in cars
and go to the A&W where teenaged girls roller skated
out to your car and attached the tray with your food
to your rolled down window. Once you got to be a
teenager, she thought, your hair would be beautiful,
your clothes would be beautiful and you would have
lots of happy friends. You would be smiling and
happy too.

– Teenagers today lip off their parents way too
    much, her mother had said. I wouldn't have
    dared talk to my parents the way kids talk to
    theirs today.

Christine thought her parents lipped each other off too much too. They lipped off to each other most of the time. But nothing really happened, nothing ever really changed. They had always been that way, since she could remember. Once she had seen Mr. Vanderveen put his arm around Mrs. Vanderveen's waist when they were out in their garden, both holding cups of coffee and she thought, "That must be love." That's what it must be. She had thought other parents were like her parents. Maybe not. In her school reader, she read a story about a family going on a picnic to Blue Pond. "Father and mother laughed," it said. Her family had never been to Blue Pond. They had been to Elk Island Park for a picnic once and her father wore his work boots and sat in the shade by himself just smoking cigarettes. She remembered it as a good day, she had learned how to swim. But she couldn't remember her mother and father as happy. They didn't laugh, not even once that she could remember. Was that unusual or usual? It would be a long time until she was a teenager, but she knew she had to make a decision. Unusual or usual. A girl in the reader said, "When I am big I shall make rhymes to put in books." Shall. What an interesting word. I shall do that too, she thought. I shall put rhymes in books and, not only rhymes, but drawings and maybe paintings to go with them. Christine made her decision.

— I shall be unusual.

She took her aunt's old Phys Ed uniform out of her
drawer. Another girl in her reader had a green dress
and matching bow, and a green purse with her own
money in it. Christine mimicked the expression
of the girl. Smiling she unbuttoned the uniform
and stepped into it. Arms through the short green
sleeves. The gathered legs of the uniform came
down past her knees and the waist fell to her hips.
She buttoned up the uniform anyway and fastened
the belt. The uniform looked more like a long
baggy dress. Christine bunched the extra fabric in
her fists and hiked up the waist to where it should
be. When she opened her fists, the green fabric fell
back down and was now mapped with wrinkles.
If she pulled up her knee socks as high as she could,
they almost met the hem. She didn't want to be
obvious about how much she liked the uniform
and how unusual she felt wearing it, so she walked
casually and quietly into the kitchen. Her mother
was washing the lunch dishes and had her back to
Christine. Her mother swished a plate in the sink
and shook the suds off it before rinsing it and setting
it to drain.

– Mom, what does Edmonton mean?

– I don't know. There was a Fort Edmonton once...

– No, what does it *mean*? What does the city *mean*
  now? What's the reason it's here? Why are we here?

— Well, Edmonton's nice and green this time of year…
   there are jobs here…

Her mother still didn't turn around and she twisted
the dish rag into a coffee mug. What could make her
turn around?

— Can I wear bare feet on the grass?
— No, the ground's still too cold. Besides, you'll get
   worms…

Her mother turned to her.

— What the hell are you wearing?
— My Phys Ed uniform…auntie's old uniform.
— It's miles too big for you. She shook the soap suds
   off her hands.
— I like it. It's unusual.
— That's one word for it. Here…

She grabbed a safety pin from a small dish beside
the sink and, with her hands still wet, gathered some
of the fabric in the back of Christine's uniform.

— Don't get it wet, Mom.
— Stand still.

The legs were still past Christine's knees, but there was now some shape to the formerly shapeless green uniform.

– Looks like you're wearing bloomers. Christine's mother laughed.

Christine laughed too and did a little dance.

– Can I take my socks off and go in barefeet?

– No, wear your shoes and socks.

– It's warm out, Mom...

– Shoes and socks. Go on...go out and play.

– I'm going to practice some physical education.

– Go get some fresh air. Get some sunshine. You'll end up with rickets.

Her mother turned away again. She wiped the counter and shook crumbs from the toaster into the sink.

– I don't want to get rickets, Mom.

– Well, you'd better get outside then...

Bonnie Prudden was always saying to keep fit, be happy. She said you wanted to avoid a dowager's hump.

Christine wanted to be happy and avoid a dowager's hump, it probably had something to do with rickets. She was afraid to ask her mother.

She pulled up her knee socks as far as she could, until the heels of her socks were halfway up her calves, and tied the shoelaces on her new, white runners. They had pointed toes and they fit her feet. Perfect for keeping fit and being happy.

Quickly out the back door, down the concrete steps and out onto the lawn. First a warm-up, so she swung her arms in big circles while running around the backyard. She could hear Bonnie's voice in her mind as she jumped back and forth over the ruts in the backyard by the garage telling her what to do while some beautiful music played in the background. Run and circle. Now making snow angels without the snow, then running on the spot, but she had to pull up the legs of the uniform over her knees. Some more arm circles then. The exercise and the idea of Phys Ed was getting boring, but the idea of wearing the uniform was still appealing. When she looked down, it kind of reminded her of an artist's smock.

While standing in the middle of the backyard she was struck by the possibilities of the white surface of the garage wall. It looked plain. It needed a painting, some kind of story. There were tins of paint in the garage. She opened the door and went in. On the shelf under the small window was a tin of red, a tin of yellow and a tin of green. There was also a tin of powder. Wood putty with that muscle man on the front. She'd used this before to make disks that held the talisman of a moment. Held them in her hands and then surrendered them to the roots of the pine tree in the yard.

Here were possibilities. Her father had a small toolbox in the corner and she rifled between the putty knives, wrenches, carpenter pencils, small hammers, boxes of nails and screws to grab a screwdriver. Popping the lids of the paint tins, the way she had seen her father do it, she laid them neatly beside the corresponding tin. There were two paintbrushes on the shelf.

She chose the widest one.

She stirred the green paint with the brush and brought it up from the tin letting some of the bright green drip back into the tin. Holding the brush like a torch, she stood in front of the blank page that was the garage wall.

Christine brandished the brush without even thinking about what was going to happen.

A triangle. Another triangle. And another triangle. There was a pine tree. She began filling the shapes with branch-brush strokes. When the brush went dry, she brought the paint tin outside. Green dripped off the brush and on to her uniform. It was beginning to look like a real artist's smock. The paint went on thickly. The tree began to sway back and forth. Its top brushed the garage roof and touched the far corners of the wall. Its branches seemed to move in a gust of wind that Christine couldn't feel and they dripped green colour all over the wall and the smell of pine shot through the air around her. She drew a straight green line on the bottom of the garage wall. That was the ground. Grass. A green clover. Five leaves by accident. She took a breath. Red and yellow. She brought out the other tins of paint. A yellow circle. The sun. A broken yoke in the sky. A red flower. Not the way she imagined it to be. This flower was just five clumsy petals and a solid blob of red in the middle. But it began to move in time to the pine tree. Now a red house beside the flower, under the sun and the pine tree.

Christine stood back and looked at what she had made. The pine tree was moving gently now and the flower mimicked its pace. The door of the house opened and people begin to walk out: the neighbour, her friend's dad, with a small smudge of red on his shoe, Brenda who's her friend, her father wearing his work boots, a man Christine doesn't know walks out of the red house holding her mother's hand, and then there is a woman Christine thinks she knows.
It's herself. She is afraid.

— Christine? Christine! What the hell are you doing?

She turns to see her mother run toward her, then she grabs the paintbrush out of Christine's hand.

— I...I...thought you'd like it. It's green...it's a green city.

Wanting to share the story of the painting on the garage wall with her mother, Christine turns and her painting and the story of the green city is nothing like what she just saw. It was simply a mess of green and red and yellow. Static, thick and messy.

— Get into the house. Stand inside the porch so you don't get paint all over the house. What were you thinking? Wait until your father gets home.

You've mixed all these colours together. They don't make any sense at all anymore...shit!

Her mother carried the paint tins back into the garage, leaving the paintbrush on the grass.

Christine walked slowly back to the house. She looked down at the uniform, it was splattered with green, red, yellow. There, on the toe of her running shoe was a smear of red. In that moment, she thought she saw herself but it wasn't herself. She thought she imagined herself moving in this house and it had been painted red, like a barn, and she was older and she was happy...no, she was sad.

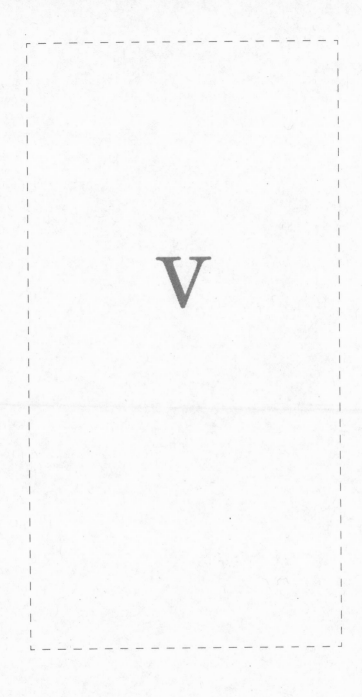

V

Christine dreams:

*A woman with a metal opening where her heart
should be.*

Around this circle of metal is smeared raspberry jam.

A dream Christine can't verify:

*She has had this dream many times and knows it
by heart, but can't get it right. A man is sitting at
the kitchen table in the old house in Santa Rosa.
He is having breakfast. The table is crowded with
people she doesn't know. And in this memory, she sees
the man chewing his breakfast. She stares. She focuses
on the veins at his temples as they inflate and deflate
slightly with each bite. Like the barely perceptible
chest movements, final breaths of a man, shot, dying
on Main Street in a TV western.*

The tree was so big now.

Christine ran her hand along its thick, cracked bark.
It reminded her of the rough disks she had made out of
putty when she was little and buried at the foot of the
tree. Hard and strong, but not immortal, not infinite.
Kneeling, she stroked the moss that covered the base
of the trunk, green fur tucked around the knuckled
roots. When she was a little girl, Christine had scraped
this crayon colour across paper turning the smooth,
white sheet into something else. Green. The colour
by itself and the smell of the colour made her think:
leaves and grass and pine trees that were green always
and anyway with fields of colour, fields grounded in
the colour of green. The bigger world of green fields
beyond this backyard, beyond this neighbourhood,
Santa Rosa, beyond Packingtown and the smell of
those meat-packing plants.

Christine had gone to the city archives, found them in
an old City of Edmonton telephone book. Her family
was in a book. Her family and herself were defined by
a street, an avenue, and a phone number. This line of
type will rearrange itself into a story of ghosts in that
place. A story of her ghost.

Christine thought of herself as a child, with no idea of the world but all the ideas in the world. Maybe this was her dream self. She wasn't sure anymore.

She had a memory of opaque light through windows in this house. She was colouring on a wooden floor with her crayons nearby and she remembered she could taste each colour. Sensation and image on her tongue. Now she could draw or paint or mold those stories that began with colour and taste, each colour had an infinite possibility of creating something, anything, everything.

Stroking the soft moss at the foot of this tree she recited other words for green: Vert. Verde. Verdigris. Celadon. Sea green. Forest green. The little house was pink when she lived there, now it was green and the open glass verandah had been walled in. Two bland aluminum windows stared out in blank surprise.

She hadn't told Fergal that she'd seen her old house listed. She hadn't told him she'd arranged to meet the real estate agent and actually gone to look at it. Same owners for the past 40 years.

It was just this tiny house. It was so much smaller than she remembered. Who lived here after them? She wanted them to buy it. The bathroom still had the same tub and sink — a hodgepog of faucets and taps, but still the same tub and sink. She would have to restore it in some way. Maybe more of an erasure than restoration or renovation. Relive or rewind. A do-over. A make-good. A try again.

This was the place she had become herself. It had made her, whether she wanted to admit it or not. Santa Rosa would always be the invisible part of her. Just as Santa Rosa was invisible now. The neighbourhood wasn't called that anymore. It didn't exist — bureaucratically, anyway. A vote to become part of the neighbourhood of Montrose. A rose by another name, another rose. A vote for Santa Rosa to disappear.

Christine is the girl that used to live here, but the girl has disappeared. Her ghost is here, existing parallel to the person she is now. How did this happen? There must have been something she wasn't paying attention to, something she didn't see coming. But the line of type in the telephone book pins her down in the north east.

She drives to the house in Santa Rosa to meet the
real estate agent. Today is a cold March day, so bright
the snow is light itself. But the house and its address
contain the ghost of its own sadness. Was this what
she carried with her for so long? The family that lived
here before and before; the family that was hers,
was gone. Ghosts.

But she had danced in that light and imagined the
specks reflected in the sun were tiny stars that shone
in the day, not at night. If she had known how to
read those stars what would have happened?

It doesn't matter which house this memory is from:
a box of cereal on the table — corn flakes, Rice Krispies —
and Christine's father pretending to hide behind it and
then peeking around the box, pretending to scare her.
It didn't scare her at all, she thought it was the funniest
thing and her father didn't have to say a word. And
most of the time he didn't. He would fill his bowl
with cereal, pour on the milk. He ate quickly. Maybe
he was just in a hurry. She thought he was angry when
she was a kid, but now she thinks he was afraid.

Her father is an absent memory. Where is his ghost?
He is the mysterious smell of cigarettes Christine
would smell late at night in the basement of another
house many years later as she sat up alone writing
or drawing or painting: the only one awake.

The CN railyard on 127th Avenue at the end of
the block her grandparents lived on let her see the
sky at night. Duplexes and houses with basement
suites; their almost hidden stairs leading to lives
led underground. This is where her grandparents
lived, a working-class neighbourhood and it
would be years before Christine even understood
what that meant. Santa Rosa was a working-class
neighbourhood too. The kind of work her father
did defined her, defined her family. Her father
took a flask of coffee in his lunch kit, and bologna
and ketchup sandwiches wrapped in wax paper.
Some Fridays, there was only puffed wheat to eat.
They didn't have the money for her father to drink
a lot back then. It was only the odd bender.

The 1963 Edmonton Henderson Directory lists
Christine's father's occupation, address, his wife's
name (her mother's name misspelled). This is a
mistake. She thinks she could have told someone.

— Hey, you got it all wrong. Try again. This isn't us.

So maybe these people wouldn't turn into her family after all and they would all get another chance.

The basement was a hole dug in the dirt under the house. Christine's mother got to it by lifting a door in the kitchen floor. She kept the wringer washer down there and once when she was rinsing clothes, Christine climbed onto the kitchen counter to get puffed wheat. Her mistake was to look back at her mother. She fell from the counter all the way down to the basement. She didn't cry and that was what worried her mother, waving lit matches in front of her eyes to make sure she didn't have a concussion.

— Watch anything you want on TV just don't fall asleep, okay? Okay?

The Santa Rosa house had a verandah and Christine loved to play out there, especially at night. The door from the verandah to the living room was open wide and she pictured her parents through it. They watched TV — *Country Hoedown* with Gordie Tapp. The square dancers wore different gingham dresses every week and were always smiling. The street lights shone on the floor of the verandah and she had put a big stuffed teddy bear her father had won for her mother at the Prince Albert exhibition on a chair.

Her mother and father are sitting close together.
They must have still loved each other.

Her mother had sewn her a dress. It was winter but
the dress was a green, spring colour and had a pocket
that was a big half-circle tilted to the side. It was dark
outside and her mother had clothes hung on inside
lines and she asked Christine's father:

– What do you think?

– Nice.

She ran around the house in the new dress and she
remembered there being a lot of room. The inside
of the house felt expansive. Standing in the middle
of a shining wood floor and knowing that one of
the doors in front of her led to her bedroom.

Once, her mother let her stay up late to watch the
fireworks. Her hair was heavy; still wet from the bath
and she stood on a vinyl and chrome chair to see the
colour and light spray and pucker and shoot from
what seemed to be as close as her own backyard.

One winter day, Christine remembers asking her
mother if she could change the channel on the TV.
It was a funeral. The President of the United States.

— This is history, her mother said.

Christine and her sister wheeled around the living
room on toy horses made of fake fur and vinyl.
She felt like a ghost, just like that president.

Christine parks beside the house. It sits on a corner lot.
The front door is actually a side door. No one seems to
live on the street anymore. No one is going anywhere,
no one is visible. The verandah has been closed in.
The curtains hanging on the windows are a series of
connected holes, variegated colours on each one. The
windows are small. She turns into the alley, backs up,
and drives around the block again.

The fence around the green house is still the same,
the gates are the same. The garage is still there, but
the glass in the tiny window below the apex of the
garage roof is gone. She painted on that garage years
ago and now knows that stories and pictures she has
created were first formed in this place. She has kept
and repeated the words spoken by the ghosts in this
house in many ways.

Christine imagines her father with a carpenter's pencil tucked behind his ear and a cigarette between his lips. He whistles when he's shaving. He tries to make her laugh. He says he feels "bluer than a cross-eyed carpenter's thumb." Christine now thinks he meant it. Her mother did laundry and cleaned the house. She smoked and drank coffee. Her nerves were bad sometimes. Christine wants to go inside because once she lived here. She has pictures of herself taken in the backyard.

epilogue

Christine stood at the long, narrow window and looked out to the backyard. The grass and the dry brown ruts from those endless comings and goings seemed new to her. Who wore those deep lines in the dirt and when? Then in the next moment she realized they had always been there as long as she could remember and probably before. Jan was in his garden, digging at the foot of the huge old pine in the back corner of the yard. Nothing grew there. What was he digging for?

She pressed her forehead lightly to the screen. The sun had just disappeared and in that instant she felt a faint touch, a coolness on her cheek. She closed her eyes. Had all of it really happened?

Her breasts were sore and hot. The nurses had wanted to give her a needle.

–   A shot to stop your milk from coming in, but she had said no. It was as if she already had been shot. Shot dead inside.

–   We'll have to bind you then dear, the older nurse said.

She was the one with grey hair and thick ankles.
Her wedding band cut into her finger. She spoke
quietly and evenly and with sympathy in her eyes.
Bind. Christine lifted her arms while the nurse
wrapped her tightly with wide strips of cotton.
Wrapped her like a mummy. Embalmed. Dry up
her burning breasts. Empty of all fluids. Empty of
everything. Her swaddled breasts. You swaddled
babies. But it was Christine who was swaddled.
Not a baby because, now, there was no baby.
What would she take home with her? She had
pictured her arms full holding a baby wrapped
in a soft green blanket. The colour of leaves the
colour of pine the colour of deep still water.

Sleeping happily. Now there was nothing. Everything
had taken so long. She must have made a mistake
somehow. Done something wrong. It had taken
so long.

– Almost there, she had heard voices saying the
  same thing.

Everyone was saying that same thing.

– Almost there.

People in masks coming in and out of the room. It was a nightmare of unidentifiable noises and masked people all in unison and moving with macabre purpose.

— Almost there.

Then silence. Nothing. No sound. No crying. What's wrong? She remembered saying that.

— What's wrong? What's wrong?

The masks turned away from her. Gloved hands were moving quickly wrapping her baby.

— What's wrong? Boy or girl? Let me see my baby. What's wrong?

No sound. No noise. No crying. Something over her mouth.

— No. Stop.

She couldn't move her tongue. It had been stuffed in her mouth and she couldn't will it to move. No sound. No noise.

Then colours in the sky.

Stars exploding in the sky. The beginning of the world. The end of the world. This is what it must have been like when the world started. This is what it would be like at the end.

– Do I have to kiss the statue? Do I have to kiss it?

– No. Not if you don't want to.

Someone had thrown handfuls of glittering sand into the sky. Sand and ice. No sound.

– Give her to me. She's just sleeping I can wake her up I can wake her up. Come on sweetheart wake up wake up for Mom there's nothing to be scared of. See look she's just sleeping. You weren't holding her right. See. She's beautiful. She's perfect. Five fingers. Five toes. Wake up sweetheart.

Christine saw all the things that might have been appear before her and explode like small stars: first smile first tooth first step first word. No sound. Where was Fergal? Christine was so tired. She saw random flashes of time in front of her. Everything that happened from her first remembering anything to this moment. Objects presented themselves over and over sometimes small and sometimes large and loud. A long white balloon. Cigarettes. Smoke. Cigarettes. Sunlight illuminating scattered crayons on a grey floor.

Yellow. Orange. Red. Green. Footprints disappearing on a shining wooden floor. The open mouth of a silver razor blade. Shining knives on grey velvet. Knives stabbing someone over and over. A movie on a drive-in big-screen. Not real. Her hands shaping small disks of putty imprinted with a feather. A little pine tree swinging from a rearview mirror. A pine tree growing in the backyard by the fence. Fergal. His face. His face. Oh so sad.

– Christine Chris Chris!

Floating in water. Green. Calm. The moon. Disappearing behind red.

Yet to her surprise here she was. Arms folded across her breasts. It seemed she could feel every pore on her skin. Feel the painful heat of her breasts. But even this was dissipating. She could change her story. Rewrite it from another perspective. Yes, she was the unreliable narrator of her own story. A liar. That was it. Somehow everything had gotten away from her. Somehow everything had escaped her. Christine would make her story turn out differently. Yes. She would do that. She wanted her story to be different.

She saw Jan digging at the base of the pine tree. Shifting his weight on the spade. Kneeling at the foot of the tree and then lifting something out of the ground. How had he managed to bury anything in those spread-fingered roots of that tree? Why would he even bother? She could see what it was now. It was a box. He lifted the lid.

ACKNOWLEDGEMENTS:

John, you've been there through it all. Thank you for that.

Thanks to my progeny, Eamon and Brendan. You were the making of me.

Mom — thanks for introducing me to the magic of nursery rhymes and fairy tales. It stood me in good stead.

Matt Bowes, Claire Kelly, and everyone at NeWest Press — thank you for your hard work on the Santa Rosa Trilogy. It's a pleasure to work with all of you.

Special thanks to Natalie Olsen whose vision for the design of *Broke City* — as well as *Santa Rosa* and *North East* — was transcendent.

Finally, I would like to thank my editor, Doug Barbour, who has been a friend and mentor to me and a champion for my writing. (And thanks for the title of this book — it fits.)

I would like to acknowledge *Broke City's* invisible palimpsest — the books, music, and films referenced, specifically or obliquely, in this novel:

Anschütz, Ernst. *"O Tannenbaüm."* (based on a traditional German folk song). Published 1824.

Clark, Barbara. "Toddle the Turtle." *We Are Neighbours — Revised Edition: The Ginn Basic Readers*, edited by Odille Ousley and David H. Russell, Ginn and Company, 1950, pp. 51–56.

Cleopatra. Directed by Joseph L. Mankiewicz, performances by Elizabeth Taylor, Richard Burton, Rex Harrison, 20th Century Fox, 1963.

Crewe, Bob, and Bob Gaudio. "Silence is Golden." (Performed by The Tremeloes). *Silence is Golden*, Epic Records, 1967.

Desmond, Paul. "Take Five." (Performed by the Dave Brubeck Quartet). *Dave Brubeck's Greatest Hits*, Columbia, 1959.

Gentry, Bobbie. "Ode to Billie Joe." *Ode to Bobbie Joe*, Capitol Records, 1967.

Haywood, Carolyn. "The Blue Dishes." *We Are Neighbours Revised Edition: The Ginn Basic Readers*, edited by Odille Ousley and David H. Russell, Ginn and Company, 1950, pp. 9–98.

Lindsay, Maud. "Fun for All." *We Are Neighbours — Revised Edition: The Ginn Basic Readers,* edited by Odille Ousley and David H. Russell, Ginn and Company, 1950, pp. 117–120.

Phillips, John, "San Francisco (Be Sure to Wear Flowers in Your Hair)" (Performed by Scott McKenzie). *What's the Difference,* Columbia, 1967.

The Family Way. Directed by Ray Boulting, performance by Hayley Mills, BLC Films, 1966.

The Three Lives of Thomasina. Directed by Don Chaffey, Walt Disney Productions, 1964.

¶ This book was typeset in Dante MT, which was designed by Giovanni Mardersteig in 1954.

Wendy McGrath's most recent novel *Broke City* is
the final book in her Santa Rosa Trilogy. Previous
novels in the series are *Santa Rosa* and *North East*.
Her most recent book of poetry, *A Revision of Forward*,
was released in Fall 2015. McGrath works in multiple
genres. *Box* (CD) 2017 is an adaptation of her long
poem into spoken word/experimental jazz/noise
by QUARTO & SOUND. MOVEMENT I from that CD
was nominated for a 2018 Edmonton Music Award
(Jazz Recording of the Year). She recently completed
a collaborative manuscript of poems inspired by
the photography of Danny Miles, drummer for July
Talk and Tongue Helmet. Her poetry, fiction, and
non-fiction has been widely published. McGrath lives
in Edmonton, Alberta on Treaty 6 territory.